TRIPLET TROUBLE
and
the Class Trip

There are more books about
the Tucker Triplets!

TRIPLET TROUBLE
and
the Class Trip

by Debbie Dadey and Marcia Thornton Jones
Illustrated by John Speirs

A
LITTLE APPLE
PAPERBACK

SCHOLASTIC INC.
New York Toronto London Auckland Sydney

ISBN 0-590-90730-1

12 11 10 9 8 7   9/9 0 1 2/0

Printed in the U.S.A.   40

First Scholastic printing, February 1997

In memory of a sweet dog and friend, Comet.

— DD

Thelma Kuhljuergen Thornton — thanks for all the great trips and for being my best friend. A better mother can't be found!

— MTJ

Contents

1

Trouble with a Capital T

Adam Tucker's hand shot up in the air. Adam is the smartest kid in Mr. Parker's second grade class. His hand is always in the air when Mr. Parker asks questions.

Mr. Parker is our teacher. He knows lots of questions. Today he was asking about things that happened a long time ago. Adam's hand waved back and forth over his head, but Mr. Parker didn't call on him. He looked around the room.

My name is Sam Johnson. I like to answer Mr. Parker's questions, but today his questions were too hard. So I looked around the room, too.

Ashley Tucker sat up straight. Her hands were folded on top of her desk. Ashley is Adam's sister. She always sits up straight.

Ashley usually has her hand up in the air, too. But not this time.

A boy named Randy sits next to Ashley. He yawned really big. He didn't raise his hand, either.

Barbara sits behind Randy. She couldn't raise her hand. She was too busy braiding the blue and red streamers dangling from the handles of Randy's wheelchair.

"Doesn't anybody know what people wore when George Washington was president?" Mr. Parker asked.

Adam waved his hand extra hard.

"Anyone besides Adam?" Mr. Parker added.

Mr. Parker waited for the red hand to sweep all the way around the clock. He looked at us and we looked at him. Then we looked at each other. That's when I saw Alex Tucker's eyes get big.

Alex Tucker is Ashley and Adam's sister. The Tucker Triplets are my neighbors. They're my best friends, too. That's how I knew Alex was thinking up another one of her brilliant ideas. I held my breath. Alex's ideas always mean one thing: trouble with a capital T.

2

Class Trip

Alex snapped her fingers right in front of her nose. Then her hand shot up in the air so fast she nearly came out of her seat. She wiggled her fingers extra hard.

Mr. Parker took a deep breath. He knew about Alex's ideas, too. He called on Alex anyway.

"Do you know the answer?" he asked.

Alex smiled so big I could see the space where her tooth used to be.

"Everybody knows what George wore," Alex said. "Clothes!"

Randy giggled and Barbara laughed out loud.

Even Mr. Parker smiled. "Of course he wore clothes," he said. "But do you know what they looked like?"

Alex smiled even bigger and pointed to her bright red jeans. "That's easy," she said. "In the olden days everybody had to wear blue jeans and plain white sneakers because colored jeans and cool tennis shoes weren't invented yet."

Mr. Parker took a deep breath. "I think we need to study more," he said.

Alex waved her hand in crazy circles over her head. She didn't wait for Mr. Parker to call on her. "I know what they ate, too," Alex blurted. "They bought hamburgers from drive-up windows because he was too busy being president to cook."

Ashley raised her hand. "Everybody knows there were no drive-up windows

when George Washington was president," Ashley said in a perfect voice.

"How do you know?" Alex said. "We should go on a class trip and buy hamburgers. Then we could ask them how old drive-up windows are. That would be a fun way to learn about long ago."

My mouth watered. Buying hamburgers sounded much better than answering

questions about ancient history.

"Alex is right," Mr. Parker said.

Adam's eyes got big and Ashley gasped. We all stared at Mr. Parker as if he'd just called off school for the rest of the year. We weren't used to Alex being right.

Mr. Parker grabbed a fat marker and scribbled on a piece of paper. I held my breath. Usually his signs mean more work.

Mr. Parker smiled and held up his sign. As soon as we saw it, we cheered. Big purple letters said: CLASS TRIP!

"Do we really get to buy hamburgers and milk shakes?" Alex asked.

Mr. Parker shook his head. "I have a better idea," he said. Then he scribbled on another piece of paper. I didn't know how to read the word on his new sign, but Adam did.

11

"I know that word," he called out. "It says MUSEUM!"

Everyone clapped their hands and cheered. Everybody but Alex. She sat very still. Quiet can be good. But not this kind of quiet. This could mean only one thing. Alex was mad.

3

Ancient History

Alex grabbed my dog's ears. Alex likes to make them stick straight up in the air, but I think Cleo looks best with floppy ears. I won't tell Alex. She thinks her ideas are the best. Cleo whined and pulled her head away.

It was after school and the Tucker Triplets sat on my front porch. Alex usually

talks all the time. But not today. She hadn't said a word since Mr. Parker told us about the museum.

"Museums are stupid," Alex finally said.

"No, they're not," Ashley said. "We'll see lots of things."

"It will be fun," Adam added. "This is the best idea Mr. Parker has had all year!"

"Buying hamburgers was a better idea," Alex mumbled. "Who cares about seeing old things from a long time ago?"

"We all do," Adam said. "History is fun. Isn't it, Sam?"

I like Alex. And I like Ashley and Adam. But when they put me in the middle of a fight, I always end up in trouble. I thought hard about what I should say. I smiled when I thought of the perfect answer.

"The museum will be fun," I said. "We'll make it fun."

Alex's eyes got big. Then she snapped her fingers right in front of her nose. "Sam is right," she said. "And I know exactly what we have to do."

"What?" we all asked at once.

Alex smiled so big I saw the space where her tooth used to be. "You'll find out when we go to the museum," she said.

Sometimes Alex's ideas get her in trouble. But one thing is for sure — Alex's ideas are always fun and I couldn't wait to find out.

Old Food

"Wow!" Alex shouted when our class walked into the museum. Directly in front of us was a huge dinosaur skeleton.

Mr. Parker turned to Alex and held his fingers to his lips. "Shhh, this is a museum. You must be quiet."

Alex nodded and didn't take her eyes off the dinosaur. "Don't worry," she said softly.

18

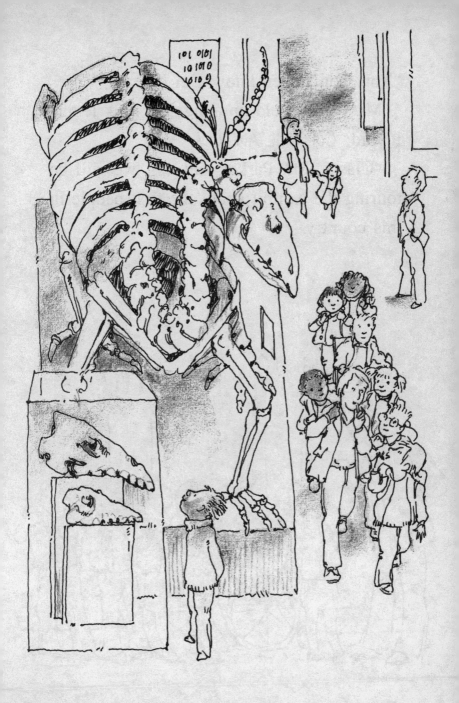

"You won't even know I'm here."

Mr. Parker held up a sign. In pink letters it said: COLONIAL AMERICA.

"Class," Mr. Parker told us, "we will be touring the exhibit about the first people in this country."

"That would be the Native Americans," Adam said.

Mr. Parker turned red. "Of course," he said. "I should have said we will be touring the exhibit about the first white settlers. It also includes a display about George and Martha Washington. Please pay close attention to what they used to wear and eat."

"That reminds me," Alex said. "I'm hungry."

Mr. Parker led the class toward a big open room marked COLONIAL AMERICA. I started to follow, but Alex grabbed me by the arm. She stopped Adam and Ashley, too.

"What's wrong?" Ashley asked.

"Studying about old clothes," Alex

21

explained. "That's what's wrong. I want to do something more exciting."

Adam folded his arms in front of his chest. "Exactly what did you have in mind?"

Alex smiled and pulled a pile of papers out of her backpack. She handed each one of us a paper.

1. Find

2. Find

3. Find

"This looks like a really bad coloring book," Ashley told Alex.

Alex stuck out her tongue and held up the paper. "This," she said, "is the way to make a museum fun. This is a treasure hunt."

I knew one thing. Alex's treasure hunt might be fun, but it was also bound to cause trouble. Terrible trouble.

Caveman

"We have to stay with the class or we'll get lost," Ashley said.

Alex pulled a funny-looking hat out of her backpack and slapped it on her head. "This is my explorer's hat. I've been to this museum three times already and I always wear this hat. I haven't been lost yet."

"I think Ashley's right," Adam said. "Mr. Parker will get really mad."

Alex pointed to the room next door. "We'll be right beside the class. There's no way we can get lost, and Mr. Parker won't even notice."

Ashley shook her head. Adam shook his head. I just stood there. I agreed with

Ashley and Adam. We should stay with the class. I started to shake my head. But I didn't get the chance. Alex grabbed me and pulled me into the exhibit marked EARLY MAN.

"Come on, Sam," Alex called. "We're going to be cavemen."

Adam and Ashley followed. "We better get back with the class right now," Ashley said.

"Just one minute," Alex said. She jumped up on a wooden display and stood beside a statue of a caveman holding a club.

"Get down from there!" Adam commanded.

Alex didn't listen. She danced around the caveman and grunted. I looked around. I

CAVE
MAN
500000BC

figured someone would come and yell at Alex. No one came.

Alex should have stopped. But she didn't. She touched the caveman's fur clothes. She touched the club. Then it happened. The club fell on her foot and rolled across the floor.

"Ouch!" Alex cried and hopped up and down. The caveman statue wobbled. Adam

and Ashley jumped up on the wooden display and caught the caveman before he fell.

"You almost wrecked the caveman," Adam snapped.

Alex rubbed her toe and sniffled. "I hurt my toe."

"Serves you right," Ashley said, putting the club back in the caveman's hand. "We shouldn't be here."

"Let's go back to Mr. Parker," I suggested.

Alex jumped down from the wooden box. "But I haven't found anything from my treasure hunt yet."

Adam and Ashley jumped down from the box. Adam pointed a finger at Alex. "Your treasure hunt can wait," he said. "You've caused enough trouble. Let's go back to Mr. Parker before something else happens."

Alex bowed her head. I couldn't see her face. Her explorer's hat completely covered her eyes. But when we walked to the door, Alex followed us.

I was glad to be going back to Mr. Parker. I didn't want to get lost. I wanted to find out about George Washington's old clothes.

I guess Alex hated old clothes, because when I turned around, Alex was gone.

6

Fountain

We found Alex. She was standing on the bricks that surrounded a fancy water fountain. A hippo statue squirted water in the middle of the fountain.

"Get down from there," Adam yelled at Alex.

Alex pointed into the water. "Just a

minute," Alex told Adam. "There's a real old quarter in there. That's on my treasure hunt list."

"Let me see," Ashley said. Ashley collects old coins. She has a whole pill bottle full of pennies at her house. Ashley jumped up on the brick wall to get a better look at the quarter. "Wow! I bet there's a million dollars in here," Ashley said.

We leaned over to look in the fountain. Ashley was right. There were quarters, dimes, nickels, and pennies all over the bottom of the fountain. It sparkled with money.

I was looking at the real old coin when it happened. It happened very fast. One minute Ashley was looking at the quarter. The next minute she fell in. Water splashed everywhere. Ashley looked like the janitor's mop from school. Water dripped from her nose, her hair, and her dress.

Ashley looked at Alex. "This is all your fault. Mr. Parker is going to kill me! All the kids will laugh."

Alex stuck out her chin. I thought she would be mad. Instead, her eyes got big and she snapped her fingers. "Don't worry. We'll fix it!" Alex pulled Ashley out of the water and led her to the bathroom.

Sam and I waited outside. We waited and waited. "What are they doing in there?" I finally asked.

Adam just shrugged. At last, they came out. Alex and Ashley both smiled.

"Ta-da!" Alex said.

I had to admit that Ashley was almost

normal. Everything was dry. "How did you do it?" I asked.

Alex pushed back her explorer's hat. "We used the hand dryer. It was a snap."

"We'd better get back to Mr. Parker before we get in big trouble," Adam said.

We all nodded and looked around. "Which way do we go?" I asked.

Alex grabbed my hand and pulled me along. "This way," she said. Alex led us up some stairs and through a hall. Then she led us down some steps and around a corner.

Adam put his arms over his chest. "I think we're lost."

Ashley looked ready to cry. "You don't know where you're going, do you?" she asked Alex.

"Of course I do," Alex said. She led us around one more corner and in front of us stood the Colonial America room.

"You did it," I said, patting Alex on the back.

Alex smiled, showing the space where her front tooth was missing. "Of course," she said.

"There's only one small problem," Adam told us.

"What?" Ashley said.

Adam pointed into the room. "Mr. Parker and the class are gone!"

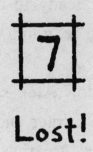

Lost!

"We're lost!" Ashley cried.

"No, we're not," Alex told her. "We just have to find Mr. Parker."

Adam sat down on the floor. "We've been left behind," he said.

I gulped. Could Mr. Parker really have left us? I felt scared. Alex made me feel better.

"Don't worry. They just went to another exhibit. We'll find them," Alex said. "Come on." Alex led us across a big hallway. There was a sign that had lots of animals on it.

"What's this?" Ashley asked.

Adam read the words on the sign. "Animal Habitat."

"I bet they went in here," Alex said, running inside the room. Alex stopped in front of a big plastic box. Five mice ran around inside it.

"Neat," Alex said, gently touching the clear box.

Ashley tapped her foot. "We don't have time to look at mice. We have to find Mr. Parker."

"Just a minute," Alex said. "A mouse is

on my treasure hunt list."

"If we don't find Mr. Parker, we'll have to hunt a way back to school," Adam told her. "Come on."

Adam pulled on Alex's arm. At the same time Alex pulled back. Alex must have pulled too hard. She fell right onto the mouse box. The door flew open!

Five little mice scattered all over the floor. "Oh, no!" I cried. "Catch them!"

Ashley screamed and jumped onto a nearby chair. Adam, Alex, and I each caught a mouse and put them back in the box. We closed the door. "There are still two missing," Adam said.

Alex's eyes were really wide. "We're in big trouble, now," she said.

"Why didn't we just stay with Mr. Parker?" Adam asked.

Ashley stayed up on the chair and whined, "Please catch those mice before they bite me."

Alex stuck out her tongue at Ashley. "Why don't you help us?" Alex asked Ashley.

"I'm scared," Ashley whined.

"Shhh!" Alex whispered. "There's one right under your chair."

Ashley looked ready to faint. Alex crawled over to the chair and grabbed the fourth mouse. Quickly, she put it back in the cage.

"There goes the last one," Ashley shouted and pointed at a tiny little mouse as it scooted out the door. We all ran to catch it.

We raced around the corner. We bumped right into a big tall man. He was holding a little mouse, and he looked mad.

8

Treasure Hunt

I looked up at the museum director. So did Adam and Ashley. Alex reached for the mouse.

"I'll put the mouse back," she said.

But Mr. Parker hurried around a corner and stopped Alex. Mr. Parker looked madder than the director. The rest of the class was gathered behind Mr. Parker.

They didn't look very happy, either. They all started talking at once.

"We haven't seen a single thing," Maria told Adam.

"We've been too busy looking for you," Randy said to Ashley.

"You've ruined the whole class trip," Barbara said to Alex.

Mr. Parker put a finger to his lips.

Everyone stopped talking. Even Alex. Mr. Parker always talks in a quiet voice, but when he started talking this time it was different. It reminded me of a cat's hiss.

"I'm sure the Tucker Triplets have a very good explanation," he said.

I looked at Adam and Ashley. Their faces were both red.

Then Mr. Parker looked at me. "Maybe Sam can explain," he said.

I swallowed and blinked my eyes hard. This class trip was turning into a disaster.

Before I could figure out what to say, Alex stepped beside me. She waved her list in the air so everybody could see it. "We were searching for the things on my list. We were on a treasure hunt."

"That's not fair," Barbara called out. "We didn't get to go on a treasure hunt."

"Mr. Parker said we were supposed to be learning about George Washington," Randy said.

"Not searching for treasures," added Maria.

Everybody started talking again. Mr. Parker put his fingers to his lips again.

Then he plucked a pen from the museum director's shirt pocket. Mr. Parker scribbled in the notebook he always carries. When he held up his new sign, the letters were very squiggly. They said: ALEX IS RIGHT!

Everybody stared at the sign. Then they looked at Alex. Alex smiled so big I saw the space where her tooth used to be.

"A treasure hunt is a good idea," Mr. Parker said. His voice was still quiet, but it didn't sound mad anymore.

Maria raised her hand. "Does that mean we can all run wherever we want to?"

The mouse in the museum director's hands squeaked. I think the director squeezed it too hard.

Mr. Parker shook his head. "Leaving the

group was a bad idea. That's why the Tucker Triplets and Sam will miss recess all next week. Besides, treasures are better when you find them together."

Then Mr. Parker made us sit in a big circle. Together, we made a list of early American treasures to find. The museum director helped us. He even let Alex hold

the mouse. Alex winked at me and smiled her big grin. I smiled back.

I was glad I wasn't in trouble anymore. Now our class trip was going to be lots of fun. Looking for treasures was much better than looking at old clothes, but I'd already found a treasure. Having the Tucker Triplets for my best friends was the best treasure in the whole museum.

TRIPLET TROUBLE

by Debbie Dadey and
Marcia Thornton Jones

Triple your fun with these hilarious adventures!

Alex, Ashley, and Adam

mean well, but whenever they get involved
with something, it only means one thing —

trouble!

◯ BBT90728-X	**Triplet Trouble and the Cookie Contest**	$2.99
◯ BBT58107-4	**Triplet Trouble and the Field Day Disaster**	$2.99
◯ BBT90729-8	**Triplet Trouble and the Pizza Party**	$2.99
◯ BBT58106-6	**Triplet Trouble and the Red Heart Race**	$2.99
◯ BBT25473-1	**Triplet Trouble and the Runaway Reindeer**	$2.99
◯ BBT25472-3	**Triplet Trouble and the Talent Show Mess**	$2.99

TT596

Creepy, weird, wacky and funny things happen to the Bailey School Kids!™ Collect and read them all!

The Adventures of THE BAILEY SCHOOL KIDS®